DATE DUE

A Note to Parents and Caregivers:

Read-it! Readers are for children who are just starting on the amazing road to reading. These beautiful books support both the acquisition of reading skills and the love of books.

The RED LEVEL presents familiar topics using common words and repeating sentence patterns.

The BLUE LEVEL presents new ideas using a larger vocabulary and varied sentence structure.

The YELLOW LEVEL presents more challenging ideas, a broad vocabulary, and wide variety in sentence structure.

The GREEN LEVEL presents more complex ideas, an extended vocabulary range, and expanded language structures.

When sharing a book with your child, read in short stretches, pausing often to talk about the pictures. Have your child turn the pages and point to the pictures and familiar words. And be sure to reread favorite stories or parts of stories.

There is no right or wrong way to share books with children. Find time to read with your child, and pass on the legacy of literacy.

Adria F. Klein, Ph.D.
Professor Emeritus
California State University
San Bernardino, California

Managing Editor: Bob Temple
Creative Director: Terri Foley
Editor: Brenda Haugen
Editorial Adviser: Andrea Cascardi
Copy Editor: Laurie Kahn
Designer: Melissa Voda
Page production: The Design Lab
The illustrations in this book were prepared digitally.

Picture Window Books
5115 Excelsior Boulevard
Suite 232
Minneapolis, MN 55416
1-877-845-8392
www.picturewindowbooks.com

Printed in the United States of America.

Library of Congress Cataloging-in-Publication Data
Blair, Eric.
Hansel and Gretel / by Jacob and Wilhelm Grimm ; adapted by Eric Blair ; illustrated by
Claudia Wolf.
p. cm. — (Read-it! readers fairy tales)
Summary: When they are left in the woods by their parents, two children find their way
home despite an encounter with a wicked witch.
ISBN 1-4048-0316-5 (lib. bdg.)
[1. Fairy tales. 2. Folklore—Germany.] I. Grimm, Wilhelm, 1786-1859. II. Grimm, Jacob,
1785-1863. III. Wolf, Claudia, ill. IV. Hansel and Gretel. English. V. Title. VI. Series.
PZ8.B5688 Han 2004
398.2'0943'02—dc22   2003014342

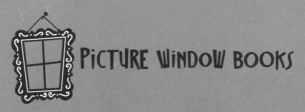

Hansel and Gretel

A Retelling of the Grimms' Fairy Tale

By Eric Blair
Illustrated by Claudia Wolf

Content Adviser:
Kathy Baxter, M.A.
Former Coordinator of Children's Services
Anoka County (Minnesota) Library

Reading Advisers:
Adria F. Klein, Ph.D.
Professor Emeritus, California State University
San Bernardino, California

Susan Kesselring, M.A.
Literacy Educator
Rosemount-Apple Valley-Eagan (Minnesota) School District

Picture Window Books
Minneapolis, Minnesota

About the Brothers Grimm

To help a friend, brothers Jacob and Wilhelm
Grimm began collecting old stories told
in their home country of Germany. Events
in their lives would take the brothers away
from their project, but they never forgot
about it. Several years later, the Grimms
published their first books of fairy tales.
The stories they collected still are enjoyed
by children and adults today.

Once upon a time, a poor woodcutter lived with his wife and two children at the edge of a forest. The little boy's name was Hansel, and the little girl's name was Gretel. The woodcutter's wife was the children's stepmother.

One night, the woodcutter was so worried,
he couldn't sleep. "How can we feed
the children when there's not enough
to feed ourselves?" he asked his wife.

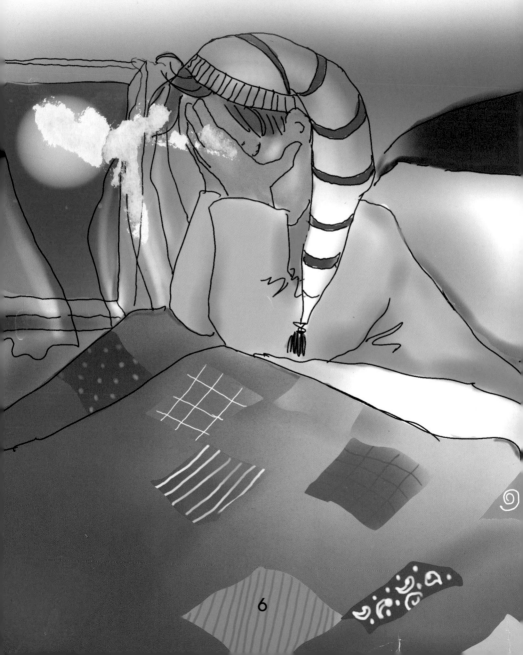

The woman had a wicked plan.
"Tomorrow, we'll lead the children
into the forest and leave them there.
We'll be rid of them."

"I can't do that!" cried the woodcutter.

"Then we'll all die of hunger," his wife said. The woodcutter finally agreed to the plan, but he felt sorry for his children.

The children heard the wicked plan.
Gretel cried. Hansel said, "Don't worry.
I'll take care of everything." He crept
outside and filled his pockets
with shiny white pebbles.

9

The next morning, they all walked into the forest.
Hansel secretly dropped his pebbles one by one.
"Go to sleep," the woman told the children
when they reached the center of the forest.
"We'll come back for you later."

It was dark when Hansel and Gretel woke up.
When the moon rose, they followed the trail
of pebbles out of the forest. They reached
their father's house in the morning.

The stepmother was surprised to see them.
"We thought you were lost and never
coming back," the wicked woman said.
But their father was happy they were home.

Soon, the cupboards were nearly empty again. "We have to get rid of the children to save ourselves," the woodcutter's wife said. "We'll take them even deeper into the forest." The woodcutter was unhappy, but he followed his wife's wishes.

Hansel and Gretel heard their parents talking. "Don't cry, Gretel," Hansel said. "Leave this to me." But when Hansel tried to go outside for more shiny pebbles, he found the door was locked.

14

The next morning, the children were given scraps of bread. Hansel crumbled his bread in his pocket. As he walked into the forest, Hansel left a trail of bread crumbs so he and Gretel could find their way back home.

When they reached the deep forest, they built a fire. "Sit down and rest," the wicked stepmother told the children. "We'll come back for you this evening." The children waited and then fell asleep.

16

When Hansel and Gretel woke up, it was dark.
They tried to find the trail Hansel had made,
but the birds had eaten all the bread crumbs.
Hansel and Gretel were lost without the crumbs.

The children were tired and hungry. When they saw a pretty bird, they followed it to a cottage. The cottage was made of gingerbread and candy. The windows were made of sugar.

The children started to eat the house.
Then the door flew open. An ugly old woman
came creeping out of the house.
"Oh, you dear children. Come in, and stay
with me," she said.

Hansel and Gretel went into the house.
The old woman gave them milk
and pancakes with apples and nuts.

After dinner, the children went
to sleep in two beautiful white beds.

The old woman seemed friendly, but she was really a wicked witch. She killed, cooked, and ate anyone who came to her house.

The witch looked at the sleeping children.
"This one will make a delicious dinner," she said,
nodding toward Hansel. Before the children
woke up, she carried Hansel into a little cage
and locked the door.

The witch shook Gretel and said, "Get some water, and cook something for your brother. When he's fat, I'll eat him up!" Gretel cried, but she had to do what the witch ordered.

24

Hansel was fed the best food. Gretel was given only scraps. Every day, the witch made Hansel hold out his finger. She was checking to see if he was fat enough to eat. Witches can't see very well, so Hansel fooled her by holding out a bone instead of his finger.

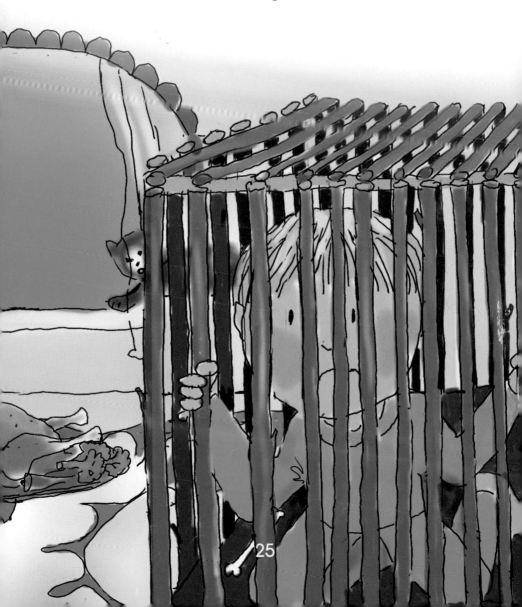

The witch wondered why it took so long
for Hansel to get fat. After a month, she said,
"Gretel, get some water. Fat or thin,
your brother will be my dinner tomorrow."

26

Gretel cried as she got the water.

27

The next morning, Gretel had to light the fire. A little later, the witch said, "Crawl in, and see if the oven is hot." The witch planned to close the door and bake poor Gretel inside.

Gretel knew the witch had an evil plan, so she said, "I won't fit."

"Silly goose," said the witch. "The opening is even big enough for me." When the witch poked her head in the oven, Gretel gave her a push and shut the door behind her.
The witch burned in the oven.

29

Gretel let her brother out of the cage.
"Hansel, we are free!" Gretel said. They found
boxes of jewels in the witch's house.
Hansel crammed his pockets full
of the pretty stones. Gretel filled her apron.

Hansel and Gretel made their way home.
Their stepmother had died. The woodcutter
was happy to get his children back.
They would never have to worry
about money again with all the jewels
they found in the witch's house.

Levels for *Read-it!* Readers

Read-it! Readers help children practice early reading skills
with brightly illustrated stories.

Red Level: Familiar topics with frequently used words and
repeating patterns.

Blue Level: New ideas with a larger vocabulary and a variety
of language structures.

Little Red Riding Hood, by Maggie Moore 1-4048-0064-6

The Three Little Pigs, by Maggie Moore 1-4048-0071-9

Yellow Level: Challenging ideas with an expanded vocabulary
and a wide variety of sentences.

Cinderella, by Barrie Wade 1-4048-0052-2

Goldilocks and the Three Bears, by Barrie Wade 1-4048-0057-3

Jack and the Beanstalk, by Maggie Moore 1-4048-0059-X

The Three Billy Goats Gruff, by Barrie Wade 1-4048-0070-0

Green Level: More complex ideas with an extended vocabulary
range and expanded language structures.

The Brave Little Tailor, by Eric Blair 1-4048-0315-7

The Bremen Town Musicians, by Eric Blair 1-4048-0310-6

The Emperor's New Clothes, by Susan Blackaby 1-4048-0224-X

The Fisherman and His Wife, by Eric Blair 1-4048-0317-3

The Frog Prince, by Eric Blair 1-4048-0313-0

Hansel and Gretel, by Eric Blair 1-4048-0316-5

The Little Mermaid, by Susan Blackaby 1-4048-0221-5

The Princess and the Pea, by Susan Blackaby 1-4048-0223-1

Rumpelstiltskin, by Eric Blair 1-4048-0311-4

The Shoemaker and His Elves, by Eric Blair 1-4048-0314-9

Snow White, by Eric Blair 1-4048-0312-2

The Steadfast Tin Soldier, by Susan Blackaby 1-4048-0226-6

Thumbelina, by Susan Blackaby 1-4048-0225-8

The Ugly Duckling, by Susan Blackaby 1-4048-0222-3